World Tree Day

From a teleplay by Norah Lally
Adapted by Susan Evento
Photography by John E. Barrett

Copyright © 2007 Mitchell Kriegman and Wainscott Studios.
First edition. Printed in the United States of America. All rights reserved.
ISBN: 978-0-696-23547-4

We welcome your comments and suggestions.
Write to us at: Meredith Books, Children's Books,
1716 Locust St., Des Moines, IA 50309-3023

meredithbooks.com

Meredith Books. Des Moines, Iowa

"Hello there," says Snook. "Did you know that today is World Tree Day? That's why I made these special badges. Everyone who does something nice for the World Tree gets a badge. Come celebrate World Tree Day with us!"

"I don't know what I can do for the tree," says Bob.
"It's so big, and I'm so small."

"Hey, Snook, happy World Tree Day!" cries Burdette.
"I knew you wouldn't forget, Burdette," says Snook.
"Of course not," says Burdette. "I made a collage to celebrate the tree. What do you think, Snook?"
"Whoa, very creative," Snook replies. "That's beautiful!"

"I would like to give you a badge for your creativity on behalf of the tree," says Snook.

"It's wonderful to be recognized for one of my many talents," says Burdette. "Thanks, Snook! I'm off to get some twigs for my artwork. Ta-ta-ta!"

"Excuse me," says Harry the caterpillar. "After my metamorphosis, when I turn into a butterfly, I will pollinate the flowers in the World Tree so they make more seeds, which can then grow into new trees with more flowers."

Snook chuckles. "Well, I think doing something good for the World Tree later is wonderful too," says Snook. "Here's your badge, little caterpillar."

"Even a caterpillar gets a badge. I can't turn into a butterfly. And I've never pollinated anything. Oh, what am I going to do?" worries Bob.

"Be careful, you don't want to break a branch," Snook warns Smooch and Winslow. "Remember, it's World Tree Day!"

"The tree does a lot of things to help us," Snook tells the marmosets.

"What does it do?" asks Winslow.

"Well, the tree helps to keep our air clean," Smooch says. "And it helps protect us from rain and sun."

"It gives us vines to swing on. And it's my favorite place to play," adds Winslow.

"For all you do for us, World Tree, we are going to do something for you. We'll clean out your dead vines to make room for new ones to grow," Smooch says proudly.

Snook gives badges to the marmosets and tells them to keep up the good work.

"Hey, your badges are great," says Bob.
"You could have one too," says Smooch.
"Just do something nice for the World Tree."

11

"Hey, Snook, I'm trying to help the World Tree too," explains Wartz. "Some of these bugs are not good for the tree."

"You're right," says Snook. "Some bugs eat the tree's bark and leaves."

"It's nice and cool here, isn't it, my friends?" says Madge. "Oh, yes it is," says Wartz. "This is great—I help the tree, and the tree helps me stay cool!"

"Here's a badge for helping the World Tree," says Snook. "Thanks, Snook!" says Wartz.

13

"Hey, Oko, are you making that wreath for World Tree Day?" asks Snook.

"For Oko, every day is World Tree Day," explains Oko. "I do something nice for the tree every day, just as the tree does something nice for me every day. I do not need a special day."

"Hmm. Maybe I could do something creative," says Bob. "I'm pretty good at poetry."

"Hi, Bob. I haven't seen you all day," says Snook.

"Actually, I've been worrying," explains Bob, "because I couldn't think of anything to do for the tree."

"That's okay, Bob. I'm sure we can help you think of something," offers Snook.

"You can make a wreath of leaves with me," invites Oko.

"Thanks, but I've thought of something myself. I've written a song for the tree," says Bob, proudly.

Bob sings his song to the tree:

Do something nice for the tree!
Do something nice for the tree!
The tree has done so much for you and for me,
So let's do something nice for the tree!

Soon, Snook and Oko join Bob. They sing and dance along.

When you're stretched in her shade
Or tasting the fruits that she's made
While the wind in her branches sings sweet serenades
Let's do something nice for the tree.

There's only one tree
That's so tall and so strong.
So give her a wreath
Or gobble a bug.
Oh, what the heck, just give her a hug!
Do something nice for the tree!
Do something nice for the tree!

We could search the whole world
And we never would find
A tree quite like this one.
She's one of a kind!

She gives every day.
We can give this one time.
Let's do something nice for the tree!

"Wow! That was really amazing, Bob!" Snook says. "Here is your World Tree Day badge!"

"Oh, I love my badge," Bob says, smiling. "World Tree, I love you!"